Faith's Journey

by Becky Cheston
illustrated by Carol Heyer

HOUGHTON MIFFLIN   BOSTON

New Worlds to the West

For all nine years of her life, Faith Westfield had lived with her mother and father in their small home in Boston. Faith would help her father in his printshop, folding sheets of newsprint into newspapers. Now she was leaving the place she had always known as home.

"What if Papa hadn't taken ill and died?" Faith thought to herself.

Faith looked out the stagecoach window at the endless grass. Boston had cobblestones and churches and schoolyards and shops. Along this road were only relay stations where stagecoaches stopped to change horses.

"Mama?" Faith asked the woman sitting next to her. "Will we like it in Indiana?"

Faith's mother kept her eyes closed and rested her head against the rumbling wall. "It might take some getting used to," Mama sighed.

Lonely and penniless, Faith's mother had answered a newspaper advertisement from a farmer in Indiana named Lucas Porter. Mr. Porter's wife had died, and he needed help raising his daughter, Ella. Faith wasn't sure if she wanted to go to Indiana.

Mr. Porter had sent a letter to Mama. The two continued to write to each other for a while and became friends. And so now Mama and Faith were moving to Indiana.

Their journey west was the path to Faith's new life—across Massachusetts, New York, New Jersey, Pennsylvania, Ohio, and into Indiana.

"Mama?" asked Faith. "Talk about the good things in Indiana again."

"Well, there'll be plenty of land and fresh air," said Mama. "And plots for gardening."

"But what if it's always cold?" asked Faith. "What if the flowers won't grow?"

Mama tried to comfort Faith, and continued. "Ella is just your age."

"But what if she doesn't like me?"

"And there'll be lots of animals."

"But what if they smell really, really bad?"

"Faith!" Mama scolded her finally. "All your *what ifs!* Don't always think the worst. It will all be okay."

Faith folded her arms across her chest and turned her face to the window.

"This journey must be difficult for Mama too," Faith thought.

Her mother was a city woman. She purchased vegetables at the market. She had never ridden a horse. Faith, at least, had taken riding lessons.

Faith decided to try one more time to think of something good about Mr. Porter's farm. She'd do it for Mama. Her mind turned to the letters Ella had written to her.

Papa has built a loft in my room, so we will have twice the space! I am sewing you a coverlet and a pillow case.

Ella's second letter contained this news:

Our dog Bess had a litter of six puppies last night! They are brown with curly tails and the softest fur ever! Papa says we may keep one for you.

On the paper, Ella had drawn a puppy with its eyes squeezed shut. She had drawn herself in pigtails and a wide smile. *That's me*, she wrote, *happy because you are coming soon!*

Faith had not written back.

A Horse Called Bone

Faith and her mother had been traveling for more than two days. According to the new driver, a man named Roger Coombs, half of Pennsylvania lay behind them. One pleasant surprise had been their transfer to a different stagecoach. This new, cushioned Concord model had softer seats.

Faith watched as men hitched a fresh team of four horses to the coach. One of the horses caught her eye—an ivory-colored beauty with a thick mane.

"Hey, there," said Faith. She stretched a hand to pet him. "Are you a nice horse?" The animal turned its head to nuzzle her.

"You like him, eh?" Mr. Coombs handed Faith a carrot. "Here—give him this. You'll be friends forever."

The horse's name was Bone. Mr. Coombs told Faith that Bone was the smartest and best-behaved horse he'd ever seen. As the coach rolled down the road, Faith craned her neck out the window for a glimpse of him.

Faith looked across at her mother. She had never seen her look so tired. And this was only the journey! How would they ever survive farm life? Their hands had never done rough work. They knew only ink, piano keys, and fine china tea pots. Faith crossed her arms and tried to rest.

Then came the first bump.

Riding Out of Danger

"Ow!" shouted Mama. She had hit her head against the seat back. Another jolt sent Faith skidding across her seat.

"Sorry about that!" yelled Mr. Coombs. "We're coming into a nasty section of road!" Then Faith heard him shout as the coach jolted to a sudden, violent stop. A wheel was caught in a rut. Faith looked out the window and saw Mr. Coombs lying on the roadside. Mama jumped out to help him.

The coach was stuck in the middle of the road. Mr. Coombs lay in a grassy ditch in terrible pain. Mama had covered him with a blanket and tried to tend his wounds. She thought he might have broken his left leg.

An hour passed, and still not one traveler had come by.

"What if no one comes?" asked Faith.

"It's the National Road," groaned Mr. Coombs. "Someone's bound to appear eventually." But even he could see that darkness was near.

"What if—" Faith began.

"Faith!" said Mama sharply. "This is not the time for your *what ifs*."

"This is different, Mama!" said Faith. "Listen! What if I took one of the horses and went for help?"

"The next station can't be more than an hour's ride," said Mr. Coombs. "And Bone, he knows the way."

Mama thought for a long time, then she walked toward the horses. She would let Faith go.

Mr. Coombs told them where to find the saddle. He talked them through unhitching Bone and saddling him up. By the time Mama hoisted Faith on the horse's back, the first pink of sunset colored the clouds. Faith rode off.

At first, Faith felt stiff in the saddle. She struggled to remember what she'd learned about riding back in Boston. But Bone knew the way, and he responded quickly to her commands. Faith loosened the reins a bit and relaxed. She felt the wind whistle by. The scents of long grass and wildflowers filled her head. The relay station was just minutes away. Soon she'd be back to Mama and Mr. Coombs with help.

Faith thought, "What if I had a horse like this in Indiana?"

Indiana at Last

It had taken just another hour for the men at the relay station to get back to Mama and Mr. Coombs, once Faith got there. The men took Mr. Coombs to the office of a country doctor. Mama and Faith rode in a wagon back to the relay station, where another stagecoach waited for them.

Two days later, Faith and her mother looked out the window at a small Indiana settlement. Faith squirmed in her seat, her legs still sore from her ride.

When they got to the station, a horse and cart stood waiting. A tall man swung a pig-tailed girl to the ground. Mama guided Faith out of the coach and over to meet the Porters. Mr. Porter patted Faith's head and took Mama's hand.

"You're here!" Ella said as she hugged Faith. "Here—we saved this one for you." She held out a fuzzy brown puppy. As Faith uncrossed her arms to receive it, she felt her fears tumble into the dust.

Faith took the puppy and whispered into its ear, "Maybe Indiana will be okay, after all."